THE BABY LEOPARD

M000096540

To Judy,

Spread the word!

Linda Goss

11/2/89

THE BABY LEOPARD

A "HOW AND WHY" STORY

by Linda and Clay Goss

with illustrations by Suzanne Bailey-Jones
and Michael R. Jones

BANTAM BOOKS
NEW YORK · TORONTO · LONDON · SYDNEY · AUCKLAND

THE BABY LEOPARD

A Bantam Book / December 1989

All rights reserved.
Text copyright © 1989 by Linda and Clay Goss.
Cover art and interior art copyright © 1989 by
Suzanne Bailey-Jones and Michael R. Jones.

Library of Congress Catalog Card Number: 89-17572

No part of this book may be reproduced or transmitted
in any form or by any means, electronic or mechanical,
including photocopying, recording, or by any information
storage and retrieval system, without permission in
writing from the publisher.
For information address: Bantam Books.

ISBN 0-553-34648-2

Published simultaneously in the United States and Canada

Bantam Books are published by Bantam Books, a division of Bantam
Doubleday Dell Publishing Group, Inc. Its trademark, consisting of the
words "Bantam Books" and the portrayal of a rooster, is Registered
in U.S. Patent and Trademark Office and in other countries. Marca
Registrada. Bantam Books, 666 Fifth Avenue, New York, New York 10103.

PRINTED IN THE UNITED STATES OF AMERICA

0   9   8   7   6   5   4   3   2   1

To our children, Aisha, Uhuru, and Jamaal
–L.G. and C.G.

For Theresa, Mariah, and Ardie
–S.B.-J. and M.R.J.

*We would like to extend a special thank you
to Marva Martin, whose artistic vision guided
us through the project.*
–S.B.-J. and M.R.J.

Storytelling is one of the trees of life. Reading and writing are its branches. Throughout Africa, storytelling is used to educate the young. "How and Why" tales and fables teach about values in life and nature.

In ancient Africa most stories were told aloud. Nowadays in modern Africa, children read stories, write their own stories, and listen to traditional storytellers.

The Baby Leopard is a "How and Why" tale because it explains how the leopard got its spots. It is also a fable because it warns us to be careful around fire.

Children from Ghana and Nigeria, two countries in West Africa, know many versions of "How the Leopard Got Its Spots." *The Baby Leopard* is an original story inspired by the "How and Why" tales and fables from West Africa.

It's story, storytelling time!

Once upon a time—a very long time ago—there lived a Baby Leopard. In those days, Leopards lived in houses, wore shoes, and told each other stories.

One day Baby Leopard wanted to go out and play. So he
asked, "Mama, may I go outside and play?"

"Oh, yes, you may, my son. But I want you to remember
one thing," said Mama Leopard. . .

3

"Baby Leopard, Baby Leopard,
Please don't mess with Fire!"

4

"But, Mama," said Baby Leopard,
"I'm not afraid of Fire. I am a Leopard.
Grrrrrrrrrrrrrrowl."

Baby Leopard ran out into the bright sunshine.
He was having a wonderful time.
He chased the butterflies.
He chased the birds.
He chased the bees.

6

The leaves on the trees and the breeze could see Baby
Leopard. They wanted to help him, so they whispered:

"Baby Leopard, Baby Leopard,
Please don't mess with Fire!"

But Baby
Leopard looked up at
them and said in an angry voice, "Who are
you? You can't tell me what to do. I'm not
afraid of any old Fire. I am a Leopard. Grrrrrrrrrrrrrrrrowl!"
    Baby Leopard would not listen.
    Instead he kept on playing.
    Until he began to smell a strange odor.
    He didn't really know what the smell was.
    Then he saw smoke.

8

Suddenly, a giraffe with a very long neck appeared from the smoke. He was very frightened. He tried to warn Baby Leopard, and so he said loudly:

"BABY LEOPARD, BABY LEOPARD,
PLEASE DON'T MESS WITH FIRE!"

  Baby Leopard laughed
at the giraffe and said, "Calm down!
Who do you think you're talking to? I'm not afraid of Fire.
I am a Leopard. Grrrrrrrrrrrrrrrowl."
  Baby Leopard would not listen.

So the giraffe with the very long neck ran past Baby Leopard. Many animals of the forest were running past him.

And soon Baby Leopard was all alone in the forest except
for one thing.

Red, yellow, and *orange* fingers began poking through the smoke. Connected to the fingers was a flaming *red, yellow, orange* body connected to a flaming *red, yellow, orange* head. And out the head came a long flaming *red, yellow, orange* tongue.

12

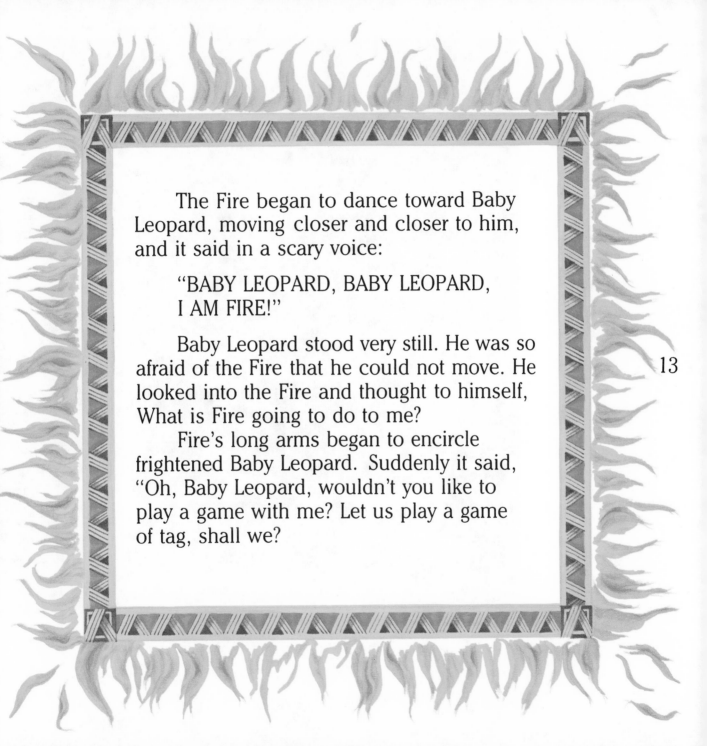

The Fire began to dance toward Baby Leopard, moving closer and closer to him, and it said in a scary voice:

"BABY LEOPARD, BABY LEOPARD,
I AM FIRE!"

Baby Leopard stood very still. He was so afraid of the Fire that he could not move. He looked into the Fire and thought to himself, What is Fire going to do to me?

Fire's long arms began to encircle frightened Baby Leopard. Suddenly it said, "Oh, Baby Leopard, wouldn't you like to play a game with me? Let us play a game of tag, shall we?

14

"*I will burn your head. I will burn your nose.*
I will burn your knees. I will burn your toes."
Scratch, scratch, scratch! Baby Leopard.

I will burn you all over your back.
Ha Ha Ha Ha Ha Ha Ha Ha Ha Ha," laughed Fire.
"Oh, oh, oh," cried Baby Leopard, and he ran home to his mama.

Mama Leopard was very happy to see Baby Leopard. She picked him up. She hugged him and rocked him. Then she put some cornstarch all over his body.

Three months passed, and Baby Leopard felt somewhat better. But when he looked at his body, he saw so many burnt places. He tried to rub them out, but they would not go away.

Baby Leopard ran out into the rain and
said, "Rain, Rain, please wash these off me."
But the rain said, "Baby Leopard, I am sorry,
I can wash your back, but I can never ever
wash out your spots."

19

Ever since that day, Leopards have had spots to remind
all of us of one thing. . .

"Baby Leopard, Baby Leopard,
Please don't mess with Fire."

22

LINDA GOSS is an award-winning, internationally known storyteller who has been featured on the *Today* show, in *The New York Times, The Washington Post, The Philadelphia Inquirer, Essence* and *Learning* magazine. She has performed across the country to sold-out audiences, most recently at the National Storytelling Festival at Jonesboro, Tennessee, the Smithsonian Museum, and the Kennedy Center. Named the Official Storyteller of Philadelphia, Goss is the cofounder of In The Tradition National Festival of Black Storytelling and the president of the Association of Black Storytellers. In addition, Goss is storyteller-in-residence sponsored by the Pennsylvania Council on the Arts and currently teaches storytelling to adults at the Please-Touch Museum in Philadelphia. In the recent past, the mayors of Washington, D.C., and Alcoa, Tennessee, (Goss's hometown) proclaimed official Linda Goss days.

CLAY GOSS is a playwright, poet, journalist, and professor. He most recently directed *The Vigil* at the Philadelphia Drama Guild, Philadelphia's major professional theater. He is the author of *Home Cookin', Five Plays*, published by the Howard University Press. He was the first playwright-in-residence at Howard University in both their drama department and their Institute for Arts and Humanities. His plays have been produced by the New York Shakespeare Festival, the Negro Ensemble Company, and the Federal Theatre. His play *On Being Hit* was one of a series of three plays that was produced at the People's Light and Theater Company and was later filmed by WHYY television for PBS; the series won an Emmy.

Formerly a contributing editor at *Encore* magazine, Goss has also written for *The Washington Post* and *Black World* as well as many other publications. Goss has also written a children's book, *Bill Picket: Black Bulldogger* (Hill & Wang).

Linda and Clay Goss have three children. They live in Philadelphia.

SUZANNE BAILEY-JONES was born in Philadelphia and attended the Tyler School of Art. MICHAEL R. JONES, also born in Philadelphia, attended the Philadelphia College of Art. In addition to being illustrators, Suzanne teaches art to young children in a private school setting, and Michael is a graphic designer. Suzanne and Michael, who are married, live in Philadelphia with their two cats, Neff and Cleo. They spent much time researching the decorative arts of Africa to ensure authenticity of detail on this, their first book.

If you enjoyed this book, you'll also like

THE THREE RIDDLES
A Jewish Folktale
by Nina Jaffe
with illustrations by Bryna Waldman